DORA & DIEGO

GIANT TORTOISE ADVENTURE

adapted by Tina Gallo
based on the screenplay written by Valerie Walsh
illustrated by Robert Roper

Ready-to-Read

Simon Spotlight/Nickelodeon
New York   London   Toronto   Sydney

Based on the TV series *Dora the Explorer*™ and *Go, Diego, Go!*™ as seen on Nick Jr.™

SIMON SPOTLIGHT/NICKELODEON
An imprint of Simon & Schuster Children's Publishing Division
1230 Avenue of the Americas, New York, New York 10020
For information about special discounts for bulk purchases,
please contact Simon & Schuster Special Sales at 1-866-506-1949 or business@simonandschuster.com.
Manufactured in the United States of America 0811 LAK
First Edition
2 4 6 8 10 9 7 5 3 1
ISBN 978-1-4424-2949-9

Hi! I am Diego.

Today my cousin Dora is

visiting me at the Animal

Rescue Center.

Do you know what kind of
animals these are?
They all have shells on
their backs.
Yes! They are turtles!

Some turtles live in the water.

Some turtles live on land.

The turtles that live on land are called tortoises.

This giant tortoise is
Lonely Louie.
Louie comes from the
Galapagos Islands.

No one has ever been
able to find another giant
tortoise just like him.

That's why he's lonely.
Don't worry, Louie!
We will find a friend for you.

Maybe we can find a girl
giant tortoise.

Then she and Louie can be
friends.

Maybe they can make a
giant tortoise family!

Where should we look?
Click can help us look for
another giant tortoise.

Click says giant tortoises live on islands.

Let's zoom through the islands and look for a giant tortoise.

Do you see something?

Say "Click!"

Uh-oh. The picture is blurry.

We have to focus.

Will you help? Say "Focus!"

Now the picture is clear.
Is this a picture of a giant
tortoise?
Yes!

This giant tortoise lives
on Lost Island.
No one has ever been
to Lost Island before.

We need to take a boat ride
to Lost Island to find
a friend for Louie!

Oh no! There are rocks under the water so we cannot take a boat to the shore.

How can we get to the island?

We can ride on Lonely
Louie like a boogie board,
and ride a wave in to shore.
Whee!

We made it to Lost Island!
Map says now we need to
climb to the top of Turtle
Rock to find a friend for
Louie!

Turtle Rock is really high!
Louie is having a hard time
climbing to the top.
Don't worry, Louie. We can
help push you up the rock.

Will you help us push Louie up Turtle Rock?
Put your hands out in front of you and push, push, push!

Wow, you are really strong!

We made it to the top of
Turtle Rock!
Do you see a friend for
Lonely Louie?

Uh-oh! She put her head in her shell.

Giant tortoises are very shy.

I will whisper to her.

I am Diego, and this is my cousin Dora.

And this is Lonely Louie.

He is a giant tortoise just like you.

What is your name?

Her name is Leslie!
Leslie is lonely, too.
She thought she was the
only giant tortoise in the
world.

Now she and Louie can be friends and start a family! Thanks for helping us find a friend for Louie!